The Treeless Plains

The
TREELESS
PLAINS

written and illustrated by Glen Rounds

HOLIDAY HOUSE • NEW YORK

CONTENTS

The Treeless Plains

1

THE FORGOTTEN
SOD HOUSES

The log cabin, along with the bald eagle, the buffalo, and the coonskin cap, has come to be a symbol
of the American frontier. Almost every Boy Scout
troop has at one time or another set out to build one
for themselves. And the architects responsible for
the structures in our national parks seem unalterably
committed to the use of unbelievably fat and well-
groomed logs for every conceivable purpose.

And until comparatively recent times a politician
who claimed a log cabin as his birthplace was auto-

matically considered to be a man loaded with the sterling virtues of the frontiersman—integrity, resourcefulness, and ambition, among others. This was not necessarily an accurate evaluation, but it seldom failed to give the lucky candidate a long advantage over any opponent shortsighted enough to have been born in more conventional surroundings.

But for some curious reason the dugouts and sod houses built by the settlers of the Middle Border—the part of the High Plains that later became the states of Kansas, Nebraska, and the Dakotas—have been almost forgotten.

Finding themselves in an almost treeless country, with no timber available for building purposes, the settlers there were forced to turn to the earth itself for shelter from the violent climate. At first they went underground, living in cavelike dugouts hollowed out of the sides of cutbanks and sidehills. Then, later, they learned to use the incredibly tough buffalo grass sod itself for building houses above ground. And for many years, until growing prosperity and the coming of the railroads made lumber

available, the sod house was as common on the plains as the log cabin had been in the eastern woodland country.

There are still a few old men who will tell with affection of these dark-walled homes of their child-hood—of the dirt roofs bright with a growth of sun-flowers, or of the mysterious gold-flecked eyes of the pet toad that grew fat on the flies clustering in the warmth of the sunny doorway. And they will tell of the entertainment furnished a lonely child by the comings and goings of the mice, gophers, and even snakes inhabiting the network of tiny burrows that soon came to riddle any sod wall.

Also, there are still great-grandmothers who will speak, with considerably less affection, of the house-keeping problems—the leaky roofs, the dirt rattling down from the rough walls or the dirt-covered ceil-ing or being blown into the house by the never quiet wind. And they make it plain that the activities of the wildlife inhabiting the walls brought consider-ably less pleasure to the housewife than to her chil-dren.

2

TIMBER
WAS PLENTIFUL
IN THE EAST

One of the first concerns of the settler or colonist in any new country is for shelter. No matter how rich the soil or how plentiful the water, wild game, and fruit, these are of little permanent use to him unless some sort of housing is available. Before anything else, he must have a reasonably watertight roof to keep the rain off his family and his meagre possessions, and walls strong enough to provide protection against the weather as well as wild animals and possible attacks by hostile natives.

But such homeseekers, whether they came to the new land by ship, covered wagon, or walking and leading a pack horse, were able to bring with them only the bare necessities. By the time space had been found for a minimum of food, clothing, seed for the new fields, and the essential tools and utensils, there was room for little else. So for the first years the pioneer had to depend on the land itself to provide not only food but building material as well.

The first colonists to land on our Atlantic Coast found timber plentiful and soon learned to build rude temporary shelters in the Indian fashion—covering frameworks of limber poles with thatch or sheets of bark. Later they built more permanent structures with palisaded walls of posts set into the ground and supporting roofs of thatch or bark. Others, framed with stout timbers, had walls of latticed branches or withes heavily plastered with clay, or a mixture of clay, sand, and chopped grass.

The log cabin, contrary to the usual belief, didn't appear until the frontier had moved from the seaboard and well back into the wilderness beyond. Then, having from necessity become expert axemen, and probably profiting from the example of the first Swedish settlers, the frontiersmen began laying up the first log huts. Tree trunks of suitable size were cut in sections somewhat longer than the proposed walls, roughly notched, and laid horizontally one on top of another to form a crib of the necessary height. Sometimes the logs were peeled before using, and some of the more particular builders even went to the trouble of cutting at least the top and bottom sides to a flat surface with an adze. But as a usual thing they were simply laid in place with the bark still on. That was the quickest way, and besides, as the logs later dried and the bark loosened, the children could be kept busy on rainy days

pulling it off and piling the scraps beside the fire-place to be used for kindling.

A low door cut in one wall and a small window in another furnished the cabin a minimum of light and ventilation; moss and clay plugged the cracks between the logs, while a roof of bark or shakes split from sections of logs kept off most of the rain.

The first floors were simply hardpacked earth, with perhaps an untanned bearskin or other fur laid down for a rug. But later, as time permitted, tree trunks split in half with the flat side adzed smooth were laid side by side for flooring. Stout pegs driven into three auger holes bored in the underside of a short section of a split tree trunk made a serviceable stool or bench.

Cups, bowls, trays, and even small buckets were carved in spare time from carefully selected burls or bits of soft wood, adding variety and numbers to the scanty supply of kitchen utensils.

By modern standards these cramped buildings with their hide- or slab-covered doorways were little better than hovels. But they were reasonably weathertight, and there was no shortage of fuel for the big fireplaces that furnished both heat and light. The land had to be cleared and the timber disposed of before any crops were planted, so the cutting of house logs for building represented no actual loss of time or extra labor.

For the next two hundred years the settlers, always searching for new land, pushed the frontier steadily westward over the mountains and out onto the wide spaces of the Middle West. And always they found timber readily available, so that with no more than an axe, a maul, an auger, and a few wedges a man could easily and quickly provide himself and his family with needed housing. The log cabin came to be a symbol of the frontier, as it is to this day.

3

THE
TREELESS PLAINS

Year by year the line of frontier settlements moved farther west until at last the edge of the woodland was reached. Then for a time all forward movement stopped.

The people were as greedy as ever for land, but they looked at those rolling treeless brown plains beyond the Missouri River and saw nothing to attract them there. On the maps of the explorers these High Plains running from the Texas Panhandle northward into Canada were called the "Great

American Desert" and declared unfit for human habitation. And here, for once, the settlers found themselves in perfect agreement with the map makers.

And it was a fact that at first acquaintance this seemingly barren land, sloping almost impercep- tibly upward to the foot of the far off Rocky Moun- tains, had little to recommend it to people long ac- customed to the woodlands of the East.

A few widely separated rivers crossed the plains from west to east, but most were sluggish, muddy streams, except in flood time, and then in a few hours they could turn without warning into raging, swirling torrents carrying a load of silt, uprooted trees, and debris of previous floods. And even in the more peaceful stages of the rivers, constantly shift- ing beds of quicksand made the bottoms treacher-

ous so that crossings were not to be undertaken lightly.

The weather, too, was much more violent than anything the settlers had known in the well-timbered country behind them.

In winter the winds from the north swept for hundreds of miles across the bare grasslands without interference, bringing the dreaded three-day blizzards and bitter cold. Of all the plains animals only the buffalo, their heads and humped forequarters blanketed by great shaggy mats of long hair, could face the blinding smothers of such storms—and even they were often trapped by the hundreds underneath huge drifts of wind-driven snow.

In summer those same winds, only now blowing from the south, brought searing heat, hail, thunderstorms, and tornadoes of almost unbelievable violence. If ever there was a land where settlers would have need of tight roofs and stout walls this was it.

Along the rivers and many of the tributary streams, where nearby hogbacks furnished some protection from storms, were scattered groves of cottonwood that could have provided logs for building as well as for fuel. But by the time the settlers arrived, Texas cattle were already beginning to replace the herds of buffalo that had once grazed by the millions on the plains. Though the cattle ran wild over the open range, access to water was a necessity, and most of the timbered bottom land had already been preempted by the stock men.

So most of the locations available to homesteaders lay out in the open, away from all such shelter. Since the scattered thickets of slender ash and boxelder in the draws and the few cottonwoods growing along the small creeks offered little in the way of suitable building material, the problem of housing seemed insurmountable.

Water could be found by digging deep wells, but these were expensive and time-consuming projects not many could afford. Any settler who didn't have the luck to find a small stream or a spring on his land would have to haul water in barrels from the nearest stream, sometimes several miles away.

So for some years more the plains were left to the Indians, ranchers, and hunters. During the spring and early summer months the people of the emigrant trains on their way to the Promised Land of Oregon and California hurried their canvas-topped wagons from one camp ground to another along the few well-worn roads to the West, looking neither to the right nor left except to keep a lookout for signs of hostile Indians. But these folk had no thought of settling here; their only concern was to cross this inhospitable wasteland as quickly as possible.

4

INDIAN TIPIS
AND EARTH
HOUSES

Even though the westward movement of the settlers had stopped at the edge of the High Plains, still more and more people came on in a steady procession from the East. Before long all the available timberland had been taken, so latecomers, having nowhere else to go, began taking a more careful look at the so-called desert.

The hunters and soldiers who had been the first to explore the region had paid little attention to the soil, but now it was discovered that under the thick mat of buffalo grass, gramma grass, and blue stem lay a deep, rich black loam. It seemed possible that by proper farming this could be made to raise good crops.

But there was still the problem of housing to be solved.

However, it was no secret that a good many tribes of Indians had long before solved the problem of living on these plains. The Mandans and Arikarees living along the upper Missouri, as well as the Pawnees and some others farther south, often built villages of huge domelike earth houses. Sunk partly into the ground, these had low circular walls of palisaded posts, which in turn supported the lower ends of long roof beams running spokelike from crotched supporting posts in the center of the circle. Other poles were lashed across this frame to support a covering of brush and grass. This done, the entire structure was buried under a thick mound of hard-packed earth.

The rounded surface not only shed rain but made

a pleasant elevated loafing place in nice weather. The dim cavelike interiors were cool in summer, while a small cook fire under the center smoke hole was all that was needed to keep the place comfortably warm even in the bitterest of the winter storms. Such a building could furnish living space for several families as well as storage for their possessions.

In some areas the earth houses were built with no entrance except through the smoke hole in the roof. This was an opening some four feet square with a notched log serving as a ladder through the smoke to the interior. But in the northern villages a doorway was usually built in one side. This not only made the coming and going of the tenants a little less inconvenient, but also allowed them to bring their more valuable horses inside in time of storm or attack by hostile neighbors.

The nomadic tribes—Sioux, Cheyenne, and others who depended mainly on the buffalo herds for their livelihood—had also solved the problem, but in an-

other way. Being hunters, moving their camps from place to place as they followed the movements of the great herds, they developed the light, portable tipi. This was a covering of dressed buffalo hides cut and sewn into a semicircular shape and stretched over a stout tripod supporting the interlocked tops of sixteen to twenty or more long poles. The cover was laced together at the front and stretched taut by pushing the bottoms of the poles outward to enlarge the circular base. At the top of the lacing was a smoke hole with movable flaps arranged to control the draft, keeping the interior relatively free of smoke. A flap-covered opening at the bottom served as a doorway.

In contrast to the flimsy canvas tents of the settlers, which, supported only by center poles, tended

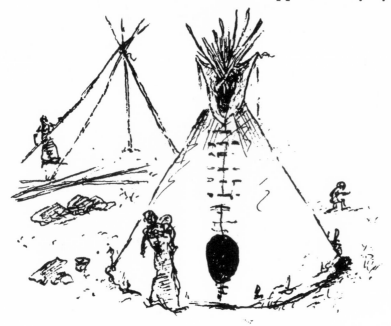

to flap and billow and blow away in high wind the broad-based cone shape of the tipi, its cover held tight by the closely spaced poles, not only shed the heaviest rain but gave little hold to even the violent windstorms so common on the plains.

On moving day the tipis were quickly and easily taken down for loading on ponies—and as easily and quickly set up again at the new camp site.

In hot weather the cover could be rolled up on the shady side to catch the breeze, if any. And in winter, with the bottom flaps banked down with earth to keep out drafts, the slanting walls reflected the heat of the small fire, keeping the interior of the tent surprisingly comfortable.

Earth houses and tipis were both simple and practical solutions to the problems of housing on the plains, but for one reason or another neither appealed to the settlers. Possibly it was because none wanted his new farm—no matter how poor and primitive—to be mistaken for an Indian camp.

5

THE
FIRST DUGOUTS

In spite of the violent climate and the absence of
timber, the prospect of free land at last began to
tempt the more adventurous land hunters to cross
the Missouri and stake out claims on the plains. At
first these settlers tried to live in tents, or in the
bodies of their wagons lifted off the wheels and set
on the ground with the bows and canvas covers still
in place. But the first sudden rainstorm more often
than not left the canvas in tatters and their belong-
ings soaked by rain or scattered across the prairie by
the wind.

The hunters and trappers, who had for years been familiar with the plains, often dug holes into the sides of steep banks to protect themselves and their plunder from the weather.

These were not really what one would call luxury apartments, but with a buffalo robe hung over the entrance to keep out wind and snow, and a tiny fire for cooking and heating, they were livable even in the bitterest weather. Livable, that is, providing the tenants could ignore the rank smells of wet furs, greasy buckskins, and unwashed bodies.

So, after the settlers had learned that their flimsy tents and wagon covers were no match for the violent winds, they too learned to go underground for shelter. Following the example of the hunters they turned to the construction of what came to be known as "dugouts." These were a little more elab-

orate than the holes the hunters made, for no settler's wife would consent to crawl in and out of her
house on hands and knees. But even so, a dugout
was a rude affair at first—simply a square-cornered
cave dug into the face of a handy cutbank. The
earth formed the floor, roof, and three walls, while a
wagon canvas hung over the open side formed the
fourth. Once that was done, the settler dug a hole
through the dirt overhead for his stove pipe, while
his wife moved in and arranged her scant furniture.
He was then free to set about the urgent business of
plowing and seeding his first fields—a matter that
could not be neglected.

But later, as time allowed, improvements were
made. Light-weight poles thrust into holes near the
top of the back wall and supported by posts at the
front carried a ceiling lattice of brush and small
branches, with grass stuffed into the remaining

overhead space to keep dirt from sifting down into the cooking and onto the beds. And the canvas covering the open side was soon replaced by a palisade of closely set poles or cottonwood logs—the cracks between them being chinked with mud and grass.

The size of one of these dugouts, housing the settler and his family as well as an occasional traveler overtaken by darkness, was often no more than ten by twelve feet, or thereabouts. But with the exception of the stove—provided the settler was lucky enough to have one—all the furniture could be carried out and put under canvas at night to make room for pallets on the floor.

More progressive and inventive folk, disliking the idea of sleeping on the floor, sometimes built portable shelf bunks supported by crosspieces set into holes dug in the wall, their outer ends lashed to upright poles. These could be quickly set up at night and as quickly dismantled in the morning be-

fore the furniture was brought in. It wasn't really an easy way to keep house, but it was better than living in tents.

So once again the pioneers had begun to learn how to make the land itself provide them with shelter. And for a time these simple, quickly constructed dugouts, in spite of their obvious disadvantages, served well. But before long it was discovered that in addition to their lack of space and generally damp and frowsy condition, these places had another most serious disadvantage. Dug as they had to be in the sides of ordinarily dry washes, a sudden heavy rainstorm or cloudburst could without warning send a wall of water racing down the steep-sided gulleys, flooding the dugouts and washing away the possessions of the owners. These flash floods usually passed as quickly as they'd come, but their short duration was little comfort to the people probing the mud for sodden clothes and bedding, or trying to salvage what they could from boxes of water-logged food supplies. So once more they began looking about for a solution to their housing problem.

6

WALLS BUILT OF SOD BLOCKS

By now the settlers had begun to learn that the tough prairie sod, held together by a tangled mat of grass roots, was almost unbelievably tough. Six horses had difficulty in pulling a plow through it, and the ribbon of sod remained kinked and twisted instead of settling down behind the plow as the loam they'd known in the East had done. It often took a season or two of exposure to the weather to loosen the plowed soil from its binding of roots and make it suitable for the planting of grain.

41

So after a few experiences with the flooding of their cutbank dugouts it occurred to the settlers that blocks of this tough sod could perhaps be used as a building material in the construction of a new kind of dugout.

Choosing a spot on a well-drained hillside they dug what amounted to a level-floored trench into the slope. This was as wide as the room was to be, and the back wall was high enough to give head room after the roof was on. Then roof beams were laid up, the ends resting on the ground at the back and on upright posts in front. These supported the ceiling of poles or brush and grass covered by a thick layer of closely fitted blocks chopped from the long ribbons of sod. With more of the blocks, laid up like oversize bricks, they built a wall across the open front of the dugout and filled the gaps be-

tween the roof edge and the slope along the sides. Space was left in front for a door, and sometimes for a small window.

These were a little more trouble to build than the first dugouts had been, but with the exception of the roof beams—which had to be hauled from the nearest cottonwood grove—all the material was close at hand for the taking. The view from this higher ground was considerably better than it had been from the places dug in the washouts, and there was no longer the threat of sudden flooding.

After a certain length of time grass, weeds, and prairie flowers grew from the sod on the roof, giving the place a gay, carefree look. Of course, when the sod roof had been thoroughly soaked by a spell of rain, the ceiling might drip for days after the weather had cleared, causing some discomfort and inconvenience to the tenants.

Another disadvantage was that the low overgrown mound of a dugout roof soon came to look like just another part of the prairie, so that the

dugout was invisible except when approached from the front, or downhill, side. So it was not unusual for range stock, or even an occasional buffalo, to graze unsuspectingly out onto some family's roof. And there were occasions when a settler hurrying home through the darkness drove his wagon over one of the invisible dwellings without ever realizing it.

If the dugout was newly built and still solid, such an occurrence usually did little damage beyond rattling an unusual amount of dirt from the ceiling. But after a year or two the beams and poles of the ceiling would begin to rot from the constant dampness of the earth roof overhead. So a family living under one of these older roofs might suddenly look up to find strange legs and hooves thrashing about just over their heads, and in extreme cases the entire animal might drop down to join them, further complicating the arrangements in the already crowded space.

Kitchen scraps, seed grain, and other bait attracted mice and gophers displaced by the plowing, and it was not unusual for one of these—or even a hunting snake—to fall from the roof edge to the space in front of the doorway to interrupt whatever the housewife had been doing there. On hot days the dark, cool interior attracted a curious variety of small creatures looking for protection from the sun. Most of these were harmless, but even so, the discovery of a gentle bull snake stretched out for a nap behind a roll of bed quilts was not a thing calculated to please the average settler's wife.

It was not particularly strange therefore, that before long a good many of the homesteaders—especially the women—began to complain that the land was not worth the price. And after a few months, or even after a year or two, the more easily discouraged gave up and returned to the East and the settlements they'd left.

But often the land they'd abandoned was taken up by a new family who moved into the old dugout, thankful not to have to build their own.

7

THE FIRST
SOD HOUSES

Some of the settler's families lived a year or two in their dugouts while they broke ground, seeded fields, and made other improvements to their new farms. But sooner or later their wives, dissatisfied with the cramped, dark, underground quarters began to demand something better.

Wood for building was still unobtainable, but there was always the unlimited supply of buffalo grass sod all about them. In the beginning the homesteaders had used this peculiar material simply as a makeshift—as people camping will use almost anything at hand for building overnight shelter. But the dark, heavy blocks had served them well in enclosing the fronts of their sidehill dugouts. Properly laid up, these walls had proved to be surprisingly durable as well as weather proof, and little by little they had come to think the prairie sod might be a reliable building material to take the place of the nonexistent logs and lumber.

Naturally there was some hesitation about taking such a revolutionary step, because many of the first small dugout walls—improperly or carelessly built —had sooner or later buckled and fallen. Not only had such a happening been a detriment to housekeeping, but it had also occasionally exposed the families to the danger of being crushed under the falling mass of dirt. But with experience the settlers had improved their methods, so before long, a scattering of small, dark sod houses began to appear on first one claim and then another.

A settler, having picked the site of his new house, waited for a clear night to stake out the corners— lining up one wall with the North Star. In the woodland country to the east the cabins, and even the more pretentious houses that came later, might face in almost any direction that fit the lay of the land, almost no attention being paid to the points of the compass. But on the plains, for some reason, men seemed to want their structures to stand square with the world, so they almost invariably lined them up with the stars.

After marking the location and dimensions of his new house the settler plowed up an area of sod close by and was ready, with the help of his neighbors, to start building. The long ribbons, perhaps sixteen to twenty inches wide and four or five inches thick, were chopped with spades or axes into uniform sections, twenty-four to thirty inches long. These blocks were not rigid like sunbaked brick, but limber like the carcass of some heavy animal, so handling them was a two-man job.

Each taking a firm grip on an end, with much grunting and straining they piled the sagging blocks on the flat bed of a wagon or on a homemade sledge to be hauled the short distance to the building site. It was no job for the lame, weak, or lazy. The first rows of blocks were laid carefully on the ground, side by side, crossways of the wall until the whole foundation course had been laid.

If the homesteader was lucky enough to have a few pieces of lumber on hand, a door frame was now set in place and firmly braced. Otherwise an untrimmed open space was left in the wall as it rose, and when the top was reached a rough-hewn log of cottonwood or boxelder was laid across the gap for a lintel to support the sod forming the low gable.

After loose dirt had been packed carefully in the spaces between the first row of blocks, the laying of the next row began, with the joints broken as in bricklaying. A careful builder made sure that every

third or fourth course was laid crosswise of the others to bind the wall more firmly together.

Some ill-advised settlers, thinking to save time and labor, built their walls of a single thickness of sod blocks laid end to end, lengthwise of the wall. But such a wall was scarcely strong enough to support its own weight, to say nothing of the dirt roof. Often they fell even before they were finished, and if not, the weight of the roof and its load of dirt was sure, sooner or later, to bring about a collapse with the danger of burying a sleeping family under tons of dirt. Even the thickest walls, unless carefully laid, often began after a time to bow and lean, requiring bracing with posts and poles to keep them upright.

Course after course of the heavy sod strips were laid one on top of another and carefully leveled until the thick walls finally stood high enough and ready for the placing of the thick log roof beam. Sometimes these timbers, six inches to a foot in diameter, were simply laid from one gable end to the

other and supported only by the walls themselves. But there was always the danger that the walls might settle and buckle under the great weight of the roof, especially in wet weather. So the more prudent set a stout post close to the wall at either end to support the ridge beam and hold the weight off the earth walls.

When the beams had been set in place, closely spaced poles were laid rafter fashion from ridge to wall and covered with a layer of hay as had been done with the roofs of the larger dugouts. At first the settlers used closely set blocks of sod for the final covering of the roof, but later they found that four to six inches of loose dirt or clay, after it had settled and packed, shed water better.

When the last shovelful of earth had been thrown onto the roof and raked and patted smooth, a piece of canvas was hung over the doorway and another smaller piece over the small window and the new house was ready to move into. These first experi-

ments were small buildings, often no more than ten by twelve feet inside, but as the homesteaders became more expert in the use of this new material the average size came to be something in the neighborhood of sixteen by twenty feet or a little longer.

No modern real estate man would bother trying to find a tenant for such a primitive structure today, and few people would even consider it suitable housing for their dogs. But for folk who for months had been living in a dugout, it was a luxury simply to be able to look out of the doorway or through the tiny window hole and see the horizon instead of nothing but the face of another cutbank. Even when divided into rooms by hanging canvas or blankets, the tiny building seemed unbelievably spacious and airy by comparison with their old quarters. And the grass on the floor, until it wore away under the constant trampling, gave the impression of soft carpet underfoot.

So it was not really surprising that the owners looked at their black squat lump of a house with a certain amount of pride.

8

PLAY PARTIES AND DANCES

With the appearance of the sod houses came a change in the social lives of the homesteaders. Travelers overtaken by mealtime or by darkness had always been welcome to stop by the old dugouts for a meal, and in emergency to stay the night. And on occasion a neighbor family might drive by to visit for an afternoon in the dooryard. But beyond that the nearest thing to a party had been a picnic in some distant grove along the river.

However, within the new and comparatively spacious houses it was possible for several families—or even whole neighborhoods—to get together.

Word would go out that a householder was having a dance Saturday night. And late on the appointed day, jolting wagons and buggies began appearing from all directions. Not only was the prospect of a party enough to bring people from miles around, but most were still living in dugouts and anxious to see one of the new houses. Both men and women wore their best, and the backs of the wagons were filled with scrubbed children, baskets of food, and even bedding, for many came from such a distance that they'd not get home until next day.

Meanwhile, the host and hostess had been busy with their own preparations. The bedsteads, providing they had them, were taken down and carried out into the newly raked yard and set up again. With the exception of the cook stove, every piece of furniture followed the beds.

The hardpacked earth floor, now cleared, was

swept, sprinkled, and swept again until it was as smooth and clean as possible. The chairs, tables, and packing cases were set about on the shady side of the shack, and all was ready for the first arrivals.

As each family drove up, their food baskets were set out on the tables beside the house and their horses unhitched and tied to the wagon wheels. While the older children stood about eyeing one another or cautiously lifting basket covers, babies were changed, fed, and put to sleep on the beds in the dooryard. Then with those things done, there was time before settling down to the supper for inspection and discussion of the new sod house—the women on the inside and the men outside.

By the time everybody had arrived and the meal was finished, and the lanterns had been lighted and hung inside and out—the party could begin. Some neighborhoods were fortunate enough to have a fiddler, but if not, there was almost surely one or two

mouth harp players in the crowd. And nearly everybody could call figures with more or less skill. If it did happen that there was no musician of any kind to be had, it made little difference, for play parties were always popular. Games of spin the bottle, London Bridge, drop the handkerchief, and others took the place of dancing. The really important thing was the party atmosphere.

So with a musician and a caller in place on a packing box set in a corner—and the cook stove, with much horseplay concerning burned hands and flying soot, finally moved into the yard with the rest of the furniture—the couples began to crowd into the room and form the sets, and the dance got under way.

These people worked hard, and when they played they played hard, so the dances often went on all

night. In that confined space they whirled and stomped, swung four-hands-round and do-si-doed.

Those who couldn't get inside clustered around the door, waiting to take the places of dancers who left the floor to cool off and get a breath of air outside.

The smaller children, after they had become bored by their elders' activity, were put to sleep on the beds outdoors with the babies, while the older ones a little later spread out blankets under the wagons or in other out-of-the-way places about the dooryard.

Towards morning, first one family and then another gathered up their sleeping children, hitched their horses, and drove off into the darkness. But others, unwilling to break up the party, stayed on. And it wasn't unusual for the last of these to stand around awhile drinking coffee and eating breakfast in the early morning sunshine before reluctantly starting on the long drive home.

9

PECULIAR HOUSEKEEPING PROBLEMS

Some of the settlers had brought bedsteads and other odd bits of furniture with them from the East, but most set up housekeeping in their new quarters with little more than a stove, bedding, and a few kitchen utensils.

However, in those days the corrugated pasteboard carton had yet to be invented, and almost everything the people used came in strong wooden packing cases of various sizes. These were handy things, serving the homesteaders in a hundred ways.

A wooden cracker box stood on end made a service-able stool—or with shelves nailed in it could hang on the wall to make a cupboard. Adding a lid hinged with bits of leather strap made it into a small chest for the protection of all manner of small treasures.

Larger packing boxes were used as trunks or storage bins. Or, torn apart and the nails saved and carefully straightened, the packing boxes furnished lumber for the building of tables, benches, shelves, bunks, and a hundred other items the homesteader needed. The wooden packing box, for some reason or other, has never been given proper credit for it's important contribution to the development of the plains.

But in spite of the improved view, the increased living space, and the added ventilation—due to having a window as well as a door—the sod houses did have certain drawbacks to really gracious living.

The interiors were dark even on the sunniest days. And after the grass underfoot had worn away,

the floors, even when carefully smoothed and packed, were dusty in dry weather and muddy in wet—a discouraging situation for any careful housekeeper to face.

In time of heavy rain the dirt roof quickly became saturated with water, which might continue to drip through the ceiling for a day or two after the storm had passed. It wasn't unusual to see the beds covered tent fashion with pieces of canvas, or the housewife holding an umbrella over her head and wearing overshoes to protect her feet from the puddles on the floor as she prepared a meal. The layer of hay between the ceiling poles and the outer dirt covering was always damp and soon became musty, which did little to improve the already close atmosphere of the house.

In dry weather, when the roof didn't leak, there were still other annoyances. Bits of earth fell from the rough surfaces of the walls at the slightest touch, making housekeeping difficult. Mice, gophers, and a dozen kinds of beetles quickly took advantage of the ease with which burrows and nests

could be made in the spaces between the dry blocks
of the sod walls—and even moved into the tightly
packed hay over the ceiling. Such a gathering of
small game naturally attracted snakes, so, what with
one thing and another, there was always a considerable amount of stealthy stirring about in the walls
and overhead—things dropping from above or scut-
tling between the walls and the bunks and storage
chests. Somehow the discovery of a mouse swim-
ming in the water bucket, or a huge beetle dropping
into the flapjack batter did little to improve a woman's temper, no matter how much it entertained her
children. Even the toads who took up stations in the
sunny doorways to grow fat on the swarming flies
were not really welcomed, as a rule.

By comparison the plight of the modern woman
whose vacuum cleaner or automatic dishwasher has
broken down seems really nothing to complain of.

On the other hand, the sod house did have many
things to recommend it. The thick earth walls and

roof kept it comparatively cool in the hottest weather. And in winter those same thicknesses of earth helped keep out the bitter cold, so the houses were not too difficult to heat.

Still another advantage—and an important one in that country—was that unlike log or frame houses the sod shack was fireproof. In a country where great prairie fires miles in width might burn uncontrolled for days, this was no small comfort to the families of the isolated homesteaders.

At the approach of such a fire the grass in the dooryard could be burned off without fear of setting fire to the house. Then, with that blackened island to divide the racing wall of fire and to keep the searing heat at a distance, the family—as well as the horses, the chickens, and even the milch cow—crowded into the sod house. There they stayed until the flames had passed, protected from both the heat and the rain of falling brands by the thick earth walls and roof.

This was by no means a pleasant or comfortable way to spend an afternoon or evening, but the lives and possessions of many plains families were saved in just that fashion.

A newly built sod house had a dark slightly rounded look—the doorway appearing only slightly blacker than the rough-textured walls, which in turn seemed to blend with the dirt roof above so that from a distance the whole affair looked more like some sleeping animal than like a dwelling. But by the second year the roots in the outside walls would begin to send out shoots and leaves, adding a gayer, softer look to the building. And on the roof, seeds carried by birds and by the wind also began to sprout. Often a small creeping plant with leaves of a soft furry gray was the first to appear there. Locally called fireweed, its bright red blossoms were an addition to anybody's roof. A pale yellow primrose was

another that made an early appearance on the otherwise sterile-looking dirt.

Later, grass and weeds took root until the entire roof might be hidden under a waving, rippling blanket of green. Nor was it unusual to see one of the older houses sporting a rank stand of sunflowers in full bloom.

But handsome as these overhead flower gardens were—adding to the appearance of the building as they did—they were not entirely welcome to the householder. The blossoms drew ants and other insects that burrowed deep into the dirt, while the probing roots loosened the packed soil, encouraging even more extensive burrowing by the mice and gophers. After a time dozens of new leaks developed where there had been none before. So eventually the plants and grass had to be pulled up and the old root-riddled dirt removed and replaced by new. The result was less decorative but much more practical.

10

THE FIRST IMPROVEMENTS

Almost immediately after moving into their new sod houses the people began to try to improve them—to make them more livable.

Before long, word would go out that someone had the first wooden door in that part of the country, to replace the usual hanging canvas. This door would be built of salvaged packing-box lumber, or a few boards bought in a spendthrift moment during a trip to town. The hinges would be bits of leather, but none the less it was a solid door, and it's owner the envy of all her neighbors.

The homemade latch was of the kind common everywhere on the frontier—a short wooden bar with one end fastened loosely to the inside of the door and the other dropping into a notched wooden block fastened to the wall. The door could be un-latched from the outside by pulling on a rawhide or buckskin thong fastened to the bar and hanging out through a hole a few inches above.

When the owner wanted no visitors he simply locked up by pulling in the latch string. Thus the words "the latchstring is always out" became an expression of hospitality or welcome.

A piece of oiled paper fastened over the small window hole was another luxury to be saved for. It didn't really let in much light, but the glowing spot in a dark wall not only gained the respect and envy of less progressive visitors, but was also a comfort to people cooped up in the cramped dark quarters dur-ing a spell of bad weather. It was a pleasant thing, also, for a neighbor to be able to step out of her door at night and see in the distance the cheerful dim orange glow of lantern light shining through the

paper window, while all the other houses in seeing distance were shuttered and invisible in the dark. It made the country seem much less bleak and lonely.

And still later, the first man to return home from a trip to town bringing a small window sash, or even a tiny pane of window glass, truly created a sensation! Whole families, on one excuse or another, drove miles out of their way to see this wonder. While the women and girls clustered around to take turns peering at the view through the window or watched enviously while the hostess lovingly polished away a nonexistent smudge on her precious glass, the men stood outside discussing crops, the latest news of the grasshopper plague in Kansas, or the possibility of the railroad's coming. When and if that happened, they agreed, prices for their produce would go up and there would be all manner of things—maybe even full window sashes, or even lumber—available at prices they could afford.

But improvement and progress, when once started, never seem to stop. By the time everybody,

except those few uncaring ones to be found in any neighborhood, had at least one oiled paper window the women began saving to buy bits of "turkey red" calico to make curtains for their windows and to hide their kitchen shelves. Others, annoyed by the activities of the small wildlife communities already established in the hay overhead, scrimped to buy muslin to tack over the entire ceiling. This not only stopped the sifting down of trash and dust but also lightened the interior considerably.

So from there it was only a step to the improvement of the appearance of the black walls themselves. If these had been left rough and irregular, there was little to be done beyond hanging a few bits of bright cloth here and there, or pictures cut from magazines, to add a little color. But many of those who had walls that had been shaved smooth set about to paper them.

Everything sold by the merchants in the towns or ordered from the East by the homesteaders still had to be hauled from the railheads by the freighters. These men drove huge highsided wagons, often

with one hitched behind the other, trailer fashion, and drawn by twelve to sixteen horses. Dozens of such outfits were on the road constantly, but a round trip from the railroad to prairie town and return might take from ten days to two weeks or more, so freight rates were high. And even though they hauled enormous loads, there was little room in the wagons for luxuries like wallpaper.

But almost everybody did have newspapers, and even illustrated magazines sent on from the East. After having been read and passed from neighbor to neighbor they were then pasted sheet by sheet onto the walls to brighten the dull interiors.

These papering projects were not always successful, since the unsized walls tended to soak up the precious flour paste, which let go its grip on the paper at the most unfortunate times. Or a spell of damp weather might bring down a whole section at a time. But with constant patching and repair these makeshifts were made to serve well enough.

Such a papered wall not only dressed up the interior beyond belief, but also served as a sort of

standup library as well. On rainy days the smaller
children could learn their letters by spelling out the
advertisements pasted close to the floor, while the
older ones searched the middle heights for pictures
and stories of faroff places—adding to their knowledge of geography while being entertained. And an
overnight guest often spent an entertaining and in-
structive hour after supper catching up on months-
old news by the light of a high-held lantern. The
thoughtful housewife tried to paste up the pages as
nearly as possible in their proper order to avoid the
embarrassment of seeing a guest frantically searching wall after wall, even perhaps going behind the
cook stove in his search for the page containing the
last part of a story begun on a page beside the window. And she naturally tried also to put the more

sensational material near the top of the wall, handy for grownups and out of the reach of the smaller children who might be considered too young for the gory details of the Roadhouse Murders.

The barren dooryards, too, received a certain amount of attention. Often a tiny flowerbed by the door was given loving care and in dry time received its share of the water hauled up in barrels for household use. But trees were what the homesteaders missed the most, and from the very beginning attempts were made to plant and protect a few shade trees. The more optimistic even sent back East for young fruit trees and hopefully set out the foundations of future orchards. But the more realistic were content with one or two cottonwood seedlings set out close to the door where they could be watered by the waste from the kitchen buckets.

Yet no matter what was done to it, or around it, the sod house remained just that—a serviceable shelter, but a thing of little grace.

11

SOD BLOCKS HAD MANY USES

Although a house was the homesteader's first and most urgent need, even the smallest farm requires a surprising number of additional buildings, fences, and sheds of one kind or another.

The homesteader's chickens had to be shut up at night to keep them safe from prowling coyotes or skunks. And nearly every farm had at least a couple of pigs bought in the spring for butchering at the beginning of cold weather for the winter's meat supply, and those had to be penned up and provided with shelter from the summer sun. Before winter, also, he must have some sort of stable to protect his workhorses and his milch cow from the bitter blizzards.

And here too the scarcity of timber presented a problem. The pig pen could be built of light poles or brush, if any happened to be handy, but having by now become reasonably expert at using the sod blocks the settler went on to build other necessary structures of the same material.

A three-sided shed, open to the south, with thick sod walls and roofed with poles supporting a heavy covering of hay, made a satisfactory stable. A similar smaller shed, the open side enclosed by a rough lattice of willow or other brush, kept his chickens reasonably safe from marauders. And in winter more hay banked against the brush wall kept out most of the wind and snow, while in the very bitterest weather a lighted lantern hanging inside helped keep the birds from freezing.

A small enclosure built of closely spaced poles and stakes thrust deep into the top of a low sod

wall and reinforced with brush made the homesteader a corral for his cow and horses, or a stack
yard to keep his winter's supply of prairie hay
safe from hungry range cattle. Providing he had
time, the settler might even build such a wall to
protect the dooryard and small vegetable garden
from his own and neighbors' livestock.

Brush and poles, when they could be found, usually had to be hauled considerable distances from
the scattered thickets along the creeks and draws, but
the tough sod blocks were always available close by
and at no cost beyond the labor of plowing and haul-
ing them into place. So in time the plains settlers
came to use this peculiar material almost as freely and
expertly as the Eastern frontiersmen had used their
logs.

In time of threatened, or actual, Indian uprising
the settlers of a community, feeling the need of
mutual protection, might band together to build a
sod fort at some point handy to the nearby home-
steads.

The simplest of these were simply thick-walled enclosures large enough to accommodate a few families and their livestock in an emergency. During the day the forts stood unattended, the people working their fields while scouts rode the surrounding plains on the lookout for sign of hostile Indians. But before dark, or in case of a daytime alarm, the entire neighborhood hurried inside the walls with their horses and milch cows, and the gates were closed and guards posted. In the event of an Indian attack the walls gave protection to the defending riflemen as well as preventing valuable livestock from being run off.

Other communities built more elaborate forts, with wells dug within the walls and with dirt-roofed shelters, partly underground, to protect the women and children from arrows and stray bullets. Some even had sheds built against the inside walls to keep the stock safe from the same hazards. Such a homemade sod fort, being fireproof besides having

its own water supply, could have withstood a considerable siege, had it been necessary.

What with one thing and another, it wasn't without reason that the people of the towns and the cattlemen living in their log houses set in cottonwood groves along the rivers began to speak of these lean people with their heavy plow shoes and clothes faded by sun and constant wind as Sodbusters.

It wasn't that the townspeople really lived in so much softer surroundings—but most did have wells in their yards instead of being forced to haul water in barrels over great distances. And some even had houses and stores built of expensive lumber freighted in from the East. The ranchers' houses were seldom much larger or lighter than those of the homesteaders, but they were usually made of cottonwood logs. And being set in a cottonwood grove they were somewhat protected, both by the trees and by the surrounding ridges, from the worst of the hot summer winds as well as the winter's blizzards. The sodbusters' shacks on the treeless plains had protection from neither.

12

NEW LUXURIES AND IMPROVEMENTS

Even after the new farms had begun to be productive, a settler—after marketing his crop and buying the necessary supplies for the coming year—often found himself still in debt to the storekeepers, or at best with only a pitifully small amount of cash in his pocket. But the women were becoming more and more loudly dissatisfied with the dark sod houses— and especially with the leaky, musty, wildlife-infested roofs. So one of the first luxuries to be hauled home by any homesteader able to scrape up the money, or able to arrange sufficient credit, was a small load of boards and a roll or two of tar paper.

The old roof would be quickly stripped of its dirt, hay, and brush, and the new boards nailed to the old roof beams. A layer of tar paper with the seams well lapped was then laid over the smooth surface and covered with a thick layer of new dirt. This not only protected the fragile paper from damage by the hot sun or the violent hailstorms, but also served to insulate the house against cold and heat, as the old roof had done.

From a distance the house with its new and expensive roof looked little different from its neighbors. But in wet weather the tar paper under the covering of dirt prevented the water seeping between the boards and dripping on the family and the furniture. And there was no longer the problem of dirt and trash—to say nothing of snakes, mice or beetles—dropping onto people's heads or into the cooking pots at mealtime.

And still later, as both money and time for non-

essentials became a little more plentiful, still more and more improvements were made. A few sacks of lime would make plaster enough for an entire room, and the smooth light walls and a whitewashed ceiling made a world of difference in the appearance of the interiors.

Naturally, the next step was to build on another room on one side or another, allowing the family to spread out a little. Even porches were added, making pleasant places to sit in the heat of the day or in rainy weather.

Of course window screens and screen doors were things still in the future, so there was brisk trade in the various kinds of fly traps sold by the stores or built by the people. Nor was it uncommon to enter such a house in the evening and find the interior filled with pungent smoke from a green sage smudge smouldering in a pan or bucket on the floor to discourage mosquitoes.

But even so, with the new improvements, the sod houses were now not too different from the houses the people had known in the East.

13

CYCLONE CELLARS AND "'FRAID HOLES"

The homesteaders soon learned that the blizzards that swept the plains in winter and the uncontrolled prairie fires, violent electrical storms, and constant winds of summer were by no means the worst of the hazards they had to face. Even more dreaded were the tornadoes—generally called cyclones or twisters. These were the violent, overgrown big brothers of the harmless whirligigs or dust devils that on hot afternoons set dust and trash swirling in erratic paths across the dry fields and dooryards.

Instead of appearing suddenly out of nowhere as the dust devils did, the tornadoes usually came in company with great black storm clouds. A black funnel-shaped tail would suddenly begin to form on the seething underside of the cloud, with the rapidly growing slender tip reaching closer and closer to the earth.

Sometimes these elongated hanging funnels of violently whirling wind writhed and twisted in the sky for a while and then gradually dissipated without ever touching the ground. But others reached straight down from cloud to earth, traveling across the land with an unbelievable roaring and leaving behind them a swath of destruction miles long and from a hundred yards to half a mile wide before wearing out their violence.

But however they traveled they were things to be dreaded. The churning, rolling mass of the storm cloud cut off the sun, changing the brightest afternoon to an eery, metallic-looking dusk. This, added to the roaring of the winds forming the funnel, made an approaching tornado a terrifying thing to

watch. And its violence and unpredictability matched its fearsome appearance.

Trees in its path were uprooted and flung down in tangled windrows yards away. A frame house might be picked up, carried half a mile or more, then set down without a broken glass or a lost shingle. Still another might be completely demolished, with nothing but a few foundation pillars and a half mile long trail of splintered kindling wood to show that it had ever existed.

Even the most solidly built sod house was no match for the destructiveness of a tornado, so the settlers quickly learned that the safest place when such a storm was in the neighborhood was underground. Thus the cyclone cellar came to be considered as essential as a house.

Some of these were no more than a pit dug three or four feet deep where the family huddled below ground level, out of reach of the wind. Others were larger and deeper, having dirt steps cut into an entrance ramp and a roof of poles and dirt providing protection from the rain and the possibility of flying debris as well as from the wind.

Still others, built even larger and deeper and provided with a door to cover the entrance stair, served a double purpose—being used as storage places between tornado scares.

In summer the cavelike interior with its thick earth roof was a cool place to keep milk, butter, and other perishables. During the long hot days of midsummer it was a pleasant playroom for the smaller children, also. In winter, with a foot or two of snow piled on top of the mound of the earth roof, the heat of a single lighted lantern was usually enough to protect the bins of potatoes, carrots, and onions.

But however it was built, and whatever the use that was made of it between tornadoes, it was always spoken of as the cyclone cellar or the " 'fraid hole." Every dark storm cloud was closely watched as long as it was in the neighborhood, and at the first sign of the dreaded funnel shape the entire family dropped whatever they had been doing and, carrying any small possessions that were handy, ran for the protection of the cyclone cellar.

Usually these were false alarms, and after hud-
dling in the dark shelter until the roaring of the
wind had died down and the sky had begun to
lighten, they came cautiously out to find everything
as they'd left it.

However, there was always the possibility that
the family might come out only to find their house
destroyed, their chickens killed or blown away, and
their clothes and furniture scattered for miles across
the prairie. So only the ignorant or foolhardy failed
to take cover at the approach of anything that might
turn out to be a tornado cloud.

The smaller, less elaborate shelters were often left
neglected and untended between storms, and this
often led to awkward situations in time of emergency. More than one family, running ahead of the
first gusts of wind leading a black storm cloud,
found themselves faced with the choice of staying
outside to risk the danger of the tornado or of shar-
ing the cramped shelter with a snake, a family of
skunks, or even a day-blinded horned owl.

14

FEW
SOD HOUSES
STAND TODAY

A well-built sod house, if properly cared for, might last for years. But such a building, due to the peculiar material, did face many hazards and require considerable attention in order to keep it livable.

The natural settling of the sod blocks under their own weight, or from the burrowings of gophers and mice, often caused the walls to shift and bulge so that it was necessary to brace them with boards and poles to prevent their total collapse.

If built in a poorly drained spot, standing water

from rain or melting snow might soften the lower portions of the walls and so bring about the crumbling of the entire structure. And dampness in the layer of hay under the earth roof encouraged the rapid rotting and weakening of the supporting beams and, if too long neglected, might bring the entire roof down on the family.

Range stock rubbing their itchy hides against the corners of the houses often wore great holes in the dry crumbly blocks, while their playful habit of gouging the walls with their horns still further damaged and weakened the walls.

An abandoned sod house was usually stripped of its door and window frames, and the range cattle quickly discovered that the dark interior was a cool shady place to loaf away hot afternoons. But they were destructive tenants and it was seldom long before the roof, with its rotting beams, either fell in of its own weight or was brought down by the collapse of the weakened walls. After that, decay was rapid. The rain not only softened and eroded the sod

blocks but also encouraged the growth of weeds whose thrusting roots caused still further crumbling of the walls. In a few years there would be only a weed-grown mound to mark the site.

But some old sod houses and dugouts—after the families had moved into their new frame houses— were given new, watertight roofs, protected from livestock, and used for many years as chicken houses and storage buildings. A few still stand today.

Few men know how to build with sod today, and even if they did, the dark crumbly walls would have little to recommend them. Of course the housekeeping problems inside could be cured by plastering, and the outside protected by stucco. But then the sod building would be indistinguishable from the modern ones built more easily and cheaply from cinder block or some similar material.

So it seems probable that the more durable log cabin will continue to stand as a symbol of the frontier, while the sod house of the Middle Border disappears altogether.

GLEN ROUNDS

Glen Rounds was born in a sod house in the South Dakota Badlands. When the railroad came through a year later, his father thought the country was becoming too congested and moved the family to a ranch in Montana where Glen spent his boyhood. After that he "prowled the country" as mule skinner, cowpuncher, logger, lightning artist, carnival talker, and sign painter, and acquired a vast fund of knowledge about many lesser-known sections and types of America.